D0540703

The Night Train

For David, Oren and Robin
– PNL

STRIPES PUBLISHING LIMITED
An imprint of the Little Tiger Group
1 Coda Studios, 189 Munster Road, London SW6 6AW

First published in Great Britain in 2021

Text copyright © Matilda Woods, 2021
Illustrations © Penny Neville-Lee, 2021

ISBN: 978-1-78895-223-1

STP/1800/0376/1020

Printed and bound in China.

The Forest Stewardship Council® (FSC®) is a global, not-for-profit organization dedicated
to the promotion of responsible forest management worldwide. FSC defines standards based
on agreed principles for responsible forest stewardship that are supported by environmental,
social, and economic stakeholders. To learn more, visit www.fsc.org

2 4 6 8 10 9 7 5 3 1

The Night Train

Matilda Woods   Penny Neville-Lee

LITTLE TIGER
LONDON

"Final call for the Night Train," the guard
yelled, holding open the carriage door.
"Express train to Sleepy Town Platform
ZZZ. No stops!"

The guard was about to close the door when he noticed a hairy white yeti lumbering across the platform. He was almost invisible against the thick snow that swirled about, except for the bright red roses on his bag.

"Good evening, Charles," said the yeti as he neared the carriage.

"Late again, Mr Yeti," grumbled the guard. "Do hurry up. We can't afford any delays!"

The yeti climbed on board and Charles
jumped in behind him. The train let out a
shrill whistle and set off into the night.

Inside the carriage it was warm and bright.
The yeti took a seat on one of the large

velvet sofas and nodded a hello to the other
passengers. Then he took a cup and saucer
and a large floral teapot out of his bag. He
poured himself a cup of tea and added in a
couple of ice cubes to cool it down.

Outside snow blustered against the windows as the train sped along the tracks. Its headlight pierced the darkness ahead and white clouds of smoke billowed up into the night. If anyone had been awake to watch they would have seen a red and gold blur hurtling through the snow.

Charles checked his watch. It was already 11:30 p.m. They were behind schedule. If the train didn't reach Sleepy Town by midnight, the special passengers would miss their chance to shine in the dreams they belonged in.

To keep his mind off the time, Charles pulled out his stamp and passenger list.

"Tickets, please!" he called as he walked through the carriage.

Charles approached the first passenger who was using the handrail as a barre to stretch his legs. He hadn't met this passenger before but he didn't have the nerves of a first timer.

"And you are?" Charles asked the passenger.

"I'm Henri." The man handed over his ticket. "At first my dreamer, Jack, made me a football player. I was the greatest in the world. Now I'm learning ballet. Tonight is my first performance. I'm dancing in front of the Queen."

"My, my. That *is* impressive," said Charles. "I hope it goes well."

Charles moved on to the next passenger. She was a small girl with a diamond tiara and a pet dragon. The dragon was blowing puffs of smoke on the window and the girl was drawing cats in the fog. Charles hadn't met her before either. He looked at his list.

"You must be…"

"Princess May," she said, handing Charles her ticket. "In my first dream I sat in a tower with my dragon, Ruby, and waited for a prince to rescue me. It was so boring. Then my dreamer, Poppy, dreamed that I escaped the tower and we've been travelling the land ever since. Tonight, we're going to the Dragon Isles to meet Ruby's family."

"It's always nice to visit your family," said Charles. He checked her ticket and continued through the carriage.

"Off on your travels again?"
Charles said when he reached
the yeti. The yeti was a regular
passenger on the Night Train.
His dreamer was a girl called
Lily who wanted to be a
great explorer. She had been
travelling towards the North
Pole for three weeks with the
yeti for company.

The yeti nodded. "Lily is not
the staying-at-home kind." He
searched among the cups and
saucers in his bag and pulled
out his ticket. An ice cube had
melted over it but luckily the
guard could still make out the
Night Train emblem and the
evening's date.

Charles stamped the ticket and handed it back with a smile. "Good luck!" he said.

"We need it," the yeti replied. "Tonight we're going to reach the North Pole, and I know for a fact Lily is going to be shocked when she sees what we find."

Charles reached the end of the carriage and looked around. There was still one passenger on his list but the other seats were empty.

"Someone's missing," he said with a sinking feeling.

"That would be me," a muffled voice replied.

Charles watched as a furry green arm
reached out from beneath the princess's
sofa.

"Argh!" he yelled, leaping into the air and
sending his stamp flying. It landed with a
splash in the yeti's tea.

"Oh no," a sad voice said from under the sofa. "I've done it again. I've gone and scared someone. Sometimes it feels like I've scared everyone in the world."

The missing passenger crawled out from beneath the sofa. It was a huge and furry monster. Henri and Princess May screamed in fright. Even the yeti looked scared. The only passenger who didn't seem alarmed was the princess's dragon, who blew a welcoming puff of smoke at the monster.

The princess was the first to recover from the shock. "I think you're on the wrong train," she said kindly. "This train is for people's dreams not nightmares."

"But I *am* in a dream," the monster said. "I truly am. Only no one believes me, not even my dreamer. Every time he sees me, Alex screams and wakes up. Then I disappear. A few weeks later, he'll dream about me again. But the same thing happens. Only it won't happen tonight because I've got just the thing to stop Alex being scared."

He reached into his bag, pulled out a red balloon and inflated it in one puff. Then he pulled out a purple and a green one... Soon the monster was holding so many balloons he started to float off the ground. "Alex loves balloons," he said with a terrifying smile.

The friendly monster was still floating about, bumping into everyone, when the brakes screeched and the train came to a sudden stop. Princess May, Henri and the yeti were flung forwards and landed in a heap on the floor. The monster's balloons popped one by one and the next second he crashed down on top of his fellow passengers with a thump.

For a moment everything was silent, then:

"Get off me!" Princess May squealed.

"Oh no! I've spilled my tea!" cried the yeti.

"Be careful!" Henri bellowed from the bottom of the pile. "My dancing legs are priceless!"

The monster jumped down, plucking a burst balloon from his horn.

Princess May rolled off the yeti and stood up, adjusting her tiara.

The yeti clambered upright and grabbed his cup and saucer.

"Thank goodness!" said Henri, gingerly getting to his feet.

"I'm so sorry," said Charles. "Please take a seat while I go and speak to the driver. I'm sure we'll be moving again in no time."

Charles opened the carriage door and stepped down into the snow.

He hurried along to the driver's cabin and knocked on the door. "What's happening?" he asked.

"Something's fallen on the track," the driver explained, pouring herself a cup of soup from her flask. "I can't see what it is from here but it's blocking the way ahead."

"Are you going to move it?" Charles asked.

The driver shook her head. "You'll have to do it. It's your job to make the train run on time."

"Isn't that both of our jobs?"

"Sorry," said the driver. "It's my job to stay here and look after the train."

Realizing he was not going to get any help
from the driver, Charles climbed down from
the cabin. Snow lay heavy upon the ground.
Treading carefully, he set off along the
track.

Back in the carriage, the passengers waited impatiently for the train to start moving. The only sound was the clock ticking as the minutes passed swiftly by. Eventually Princess May spoke.

"Do you think we should help?" she asked.

None of the other passengers answered. Henri was busy running through his dance moves, the yeti was pouring himself another cup of tea and the monster was frantically blowing up more balloons.

"Fine," said Princess May, getting to her feet. "I'll go by myself. Come on, Ruby."

Ruby flew on to Princess May's shoulder.
With a final glare at the other passengers,
the princess opened the carriage door and
jumped down into the snow. She followed
the trail of footprints until she found
Charles who was standing at the front of
the train.

The train had stopped on the edge of a
narrow bridge spanning a deep gorge.
Princess May looked around. Mountains
heavy with snow loomed high above. Then
she saw a large tree lying across the track
up ahead. It must have tumbled down the
slopes, felled by the weight of the snow.

"Can you move it?" asked Princess May. "I don't want to miss Poppy's dream. And Ruby's very excited about meeting her dragon family."

"Afraid not," said Charles. "It's much too heavy for me to lift. I'm sorry. You won't reach your dreams tonight."

"Maybe the other passengers could help?" Princess May suggested.

Charles shook his head. "Oh no, you're all far too important to help with this."

"None of us will be important if we don't make it to Sleepy Town," replied the princess a little crossly. "Come on."

Charles hurried after the princess back to the train. They climbed up into the carriage and turned to the waiting passengers.

"Charles needs our help!" said Princess May.

"A tree's fallen across the track," Charles explained. "I can't move it on my own."

"It's not our problem," said the monster. "And anyway, I've got to blow up more balloons for Alex."

"And I can't risk injuring myself," said Henri. "You need to sort this out. I must get to my dream. I can't leave the Queen waiting and Jack will be devastated if I miss the performance."

"And what about Lily?" said the yeti.
"She's not brave enough to continue our
adventure alone."

Charles looked at his watch. Time was
running out.

"Well, that's that then," he said sadly. "I'm
afraid four dreams will be empty tonight."

The stress of the night became too much
and he collapsed on to one of the sofas.

The princess stared at the passengers in disbelief. "Now look what you've done."

"We didn't do anything," the yeti said defensively.

"Exactly!" yelled Princess May. "We all want to get to our dreams tonight – they're all important – but what about Charles's dream? He just wants to get us to Sleepy Town on time. Why can't we help him?"

"How could we help?" asked Henri. "I only know how to score goals and do ten pirouettes in a row."

"And I only know how to make icy tea," the yeti pointed out.

"And I'm just good at scaring people," the monster said sadly. "Even when I don't want to."

"We've all got more skills than that," said Princess May. "We just haven't discovered them. I spent twenty nights sitting in a castle waiting for a prince to rescue me before I realized I could rescue myself. Come on. Let's go and see what we can do."

The passengers looked at one another.
They seemed unsure but hopeful. Maybe
the princess was right. Maybe they could
do more than they thought.

Leaving Charles to recover they hurried out of the carriage.

They followed the track through the snow until they reached the bridge.

Princess May pointed to the fallen tree. "That's what we have to fix." She looked to the other passengers for ideas about how they could help.

"I suppose with my balance," said Henri,
"I could walk along the track to the fallen
tree. But I'm not strong enough to move it."

"I am," the yeti said. He'd brought his cup
of tea with him and paused to take a sip.
"But I'm too wobbly to make it out there."

"You could use this," said the monster.
He held up the pieces of rope he used to
tie his balloons together. "Henri could walk
out to the tree and tie the rope around the
trunk. And you, Mr Yeti, could pull it off
the track."

"But what about the stage lights?" Henri said. "I can only perform when the lights are bright and there are no lights out there." He pointed to the blackened world that stretched out before them.

"Don't worry," Princess May said. "I'll take care of that."

The princess and Ruby hurried back to the train and knocked on the cabin door. The driver was keeping warm by the dwindling fire.

"Could you put the headlight back on?" the princess asked.

The driver shook her head. "We don't have enough power."

"I can help!" Princess May opened the
firebox and Ruby blew huge gusts of fire
on to the coal. Instantly the headlight grew
brighter, lighting up the track ahead.

As the world lit up around him, so did Henri's face.

"To your places!" he called. If they moved quickly, he might star in two performances tonight instead of one.

The monster finished tying the lengths of rope together and handed it to Henri.

The yeti lumbered over to wish him good luck.

Then Henri slowly began to walk out across
the bridge.

Walking on a track in the snow was a lot trickier than walking on the stage. A few times Henri almost lost his balance. But eventually he reached the fallen tree and tied the rope around it.

"Ready? Pull!" he called back to the yeti.

The yeti put down his cup of tea and began to pull on the rope.

"I don't think I can do it," he said through gritted teeth. "It's too heavy, even for me."

"I'll help," the monster offered. He wrapped his giant green arms around the yeti and pulled.

Slowly the tree began to move. It rolled
along the track for a short while before
falling over the edge into the valley below.
The yeti let go of the rope just in time.

"We did it!" the yeti cried. He was so excited he kicked over his cup of tea and didn't even care.

"And you didn't flinch when I touched you!" The monster smiled. His own dream had just come true.

"Did you see how good I was?" Henri ran to join them. "I balanced like a pro! I stole the show! I saved the day, or should I say the night?"

"You were all marvellous!" Princess May called. "Now, come on! We just might make it to Sleepy Town after all."

The passengers hurried back along the
track and clambered aboard. The train let
out a cheerful whistle, as if thanking them,
and set off into the night.

Charles felt the train move and slowly
opened his eyes.

"You did it," he said to the passengers.

Princess May nodded. "We all worked together," she said.

"And now we might make it to our dreams in time," the monster added, pointing to the clock.

"Thank you," Charles said with a relieved smile.

"You did a fine job with that balancing," the yeti said to Henri as the train hurtled across the bridge. "Could you give me some tips? It might come in handy if Lily and I traverse a ravine one day."

"Of course," said Henri. "It's all in the knees."

"And can you teach me how to tie knots?" Princess May asked the monster. "If Poppy ever imagines me into another castle, I'll have no problem escaping!"

The passengers were so busy talking they didn't even realize when the train pulled in to Platform ZZZ. There was just one minute to spare.

"Quickly!" said
Charles, opening
the carriage door.
"Off you go. Don't
delay. The clock's about
to chime twelve."

The passengers hurried off the train.

"Goodbye!" called Princess May with a wave. Ruby, perched on the princess's shoulder, flapped her wings in farewell.

"Until next time!" the yeti yelled. "I hope we meet again soon!"

"Wish me luck," said Henri as he danced down the platform.

"And me too!" the monster cried. He'd blown up so many balloons he was beginning to fly away. Henri leaped into the air and pulled him back down.

"I don't think you're scary at all," the ballet dancer said.

"Really?" The monster grinned a truly terrifying grin.

"Really!" said Henri. Then he faded from the platform as he entered Jack's dream and headed for the royal palace.

Princess May and Ruby disappeared too.
In a moment they would reach the Dragon
Isles.

The yeti lumbered his way into Lily's
dream, ready with two cups of icy tea.

Last to enter his dreamer's dream was the friendly monster. He took a deep breath, checked that he had enough balloons and then flew down into Alex's dream. Hopefully tonight was the night that Alex would finally not be afraid.

Charles smiled as the platform emptied. He blew his whistle and the Night Train pulled out of the station. Despite the unexpected stop it had been a successful journey. All the children in Sleepy Town would have sweet dreams tonight.

The End